THE WIND IN THE WILLOWS

The Wild Wood

Re-told by Anne McKie. Illustrated by Ken McKie.

The Mole had long wanted to meet Mr. Badger. He seemed such an important fellow. Everyone knew of him but hardly ever saw him.

"Badger will turn up some day or another, and then I'll introduce you!" promised the Rat.

"Couldn't you ask him here to dinner or something?" said the Mole.

"He wouldn't come," replied the Rat simply. "Badger hates coming to dinner, and all that sort of thing."

"Well, then, supposing we go and call on him?" suggested the Mole.

"Oh, I'm sure he wouldn't like that at all!" said the Rat, quite alarmed. "Besides, we can't, because he lives in the very middle of the Wild Wood! He'll come here some day, if you wait long enough."

But Badger never did come. The summer was long over and winter was on its way. Mole waited and waited, still longing to meet this mysterious grey Badger who lived by himself in the middle of the Wild Wood.

So it was, that on one winter's day, when the Mole had a good deal of spare time on his hands, that he decided to go out by himself and explore the Wild Wood - and perhaps meet Mr. Badger.

The Rat was dozing in his armchair in front of a blazing fire when Mole slipped quietly out of the warm parlour and into the open air.

The afternoon sky was cold and grey and the countryside bare and leafless. Mole had never been so far before and he was beginning to quite enjoy the different look of the fields and trees in winter.

In fact he felt very cheerful as he pushed on towards the Wild Wood, which lay before him low and threatening.

There was nothing to frighten him at first. Twigs crackled under his feet, logs tripped him, fungi on stumps looked like faces and startled him for a moment; but that was all fun and exciting. It led him on, and he went deeper into the wood where the light was less and the trees made ugly frightening shapes.

Everything was very still now. Dusk was falling and, little by little, the light was fading.

Then the faces began. First a little evil wedge-shaped face, looking out at him from a hole - then vanishing.

He quickened his pace, telling himself cheerfully not to begin imagining things!

Then suddenly, Mole seemed to see a face in every hole; hundreds of them staring at him with evil hard eyes. Quickly he dived off the path and plunged deep into the wood itself.

Then the whistling began. Very faint and shrill it was, and far behind him - the Mole hurried forward - and there it was again - in front of him this time. Poor Mole was quite alone, far from help and the night was closing in.

Then the pattering began. He thought it was only falling leaves at first! But no! It seemed to be the pat-pat-pat of little feet. Was it in front or behind?

As he stood still to listen, a rabbit came running hard towards him, "Get out of this, you fool, get out!" the Mole heard him mutter as he swung round a stump and disappeared down a friendly burrow.

The pattering increased. The whole wood seemed to be running now and closing in around poor Mole.

In panic, he began to run too. He bumped into things, fell
over things and darted under things. At last he hid in the deep,
dark hollow of an old beech tree.

As he lay there panting and trembling and listening to the
whistlings and patterings outside he knew, at last, the thing that
Ratty had tried to keep him away from: the Terror of the Wild
Wood!

Meanwhile, the Rat, warm and comfortable, dozed by his
fireside. Then a coal slipped, the fire crackled and sent up a spurt
of flame and he awoke with a start.

He looked round for Mole, but
Mole was not there! He listened for a
while. The house seemed very quiet.

Then he called "Moley!"
several times, and, getting no answer,
got up and went into the hall.

The Mole's cap was missing
from its peg, and his galoshes were
also gone.

Rat left the house and found
Mole's footprints outside in the mud
leading straight to the Wild Wood.

The Rat looked very grave. Then he went back into his house, strapped a belt round his waist, shoved a pair of pistols into it, took a stout stick, and set off for the Wild Wood at a smart pace!

It was already getting dark when he reached the first fringe of trees. Straight away he rushed deep into the wood looking for any sign of the Mole.

Here and there wicked little faces popped out of holes, but vanished at the sight of the brave Water Rat. The whistling and pattering died away, and all was very still.

The Rat made his way through the dark wood, all the time calling out cheerfully, "Moley! Moley! Moley! Where are you? It's me - it's old Rat!"

Then at last to his joy, he heard a little answering cry. From out of a hole in an old beech tree came a feeble voice saying, "Ratty, is that really you?"

The Rat crept into the hollow and there he found the Mole, exhausted and still trembling. "Oh, Rat!" he cried, "I've been so frightened, you can't think!"

The Mole was greatly cheered up by the sight of the Rat's stick and his gleaming pistols, and he stopped shivering and began to feel bolder and more himself again.

"Now then," said the Rat presently, "we really must start for home while there's still a little light left. It would never do to spend the night here!"

"Dear Ratty," said the poor Mole, "I'm simply dead beat. You must let me rest a while and get my strength back."

"Oh, alright," said the good-natured Rat, "rest away, it's nearly pitch dark now anyhow, and there ought to be a bit of moon later."

So the Mole stretched himself out on the dry leaves and went to sleep while the Rat lay patiently waiting, with a pistol in his paw.

When at last the Mole woke up, the Rat said, "I'll take a look outside, then we really must be off."

The Rat went to the entrance of their hollow tree. Then the Mole heard him say quietly to himself, "Hello! Hello! Well I never!"

"What's up, Ratty?" asked the Mole.

"Snow is up," replied the Rat briefly, "or rather, down! It's snowing hard."

A gleaming carpet of snow was springing up everywhere, filling the air with its fine, delicate powder.

"We must make a start," said the Rat. "The worst of it is, I don't know exactly where we are and this snow makes everything look so different."

It did indeed! However they set out bravely, trying to find the right path.

An hour or two later, they had lost all track of time - they pulled up, downhearted, weary and hopelessly lost!

They were aching and bruised with tumbles; they had fallen into several holes and got wet through. The snow was getting so deep that they could hardly drag their little legs through it.

"We can't sit here very long," said the Rat. "We must try to find a cave or a hole with a dry floor, out of the wind and the snow!"

So, once more they got to their feet and struggled on through the whirling snow, when, suddenly, Mole tripped up and fell forward on his face with a groan. "Oh, my leg," he cried. "Oh, my poor shin!" and he sat up on the snow and nursed his leg in both front paws. "I must have tripped over a hidden branch or a stump," went on the Mole miserably.

"That was never done by a branch or stump," said Ratty examining the Mole's leg. "Looks as if it was made by a sharp metal edge. Funny!"

"It hurts just the same, whatever done it!" cried poor Mole as the Rat carefully tied up the leg with his handkerchief.

Then to Mole's surprise, the Rat began to scratch and shovel the snow. Suddenly, the Rat cried, "Hooray! Hooray!" and danced a jig in the snow. "Come and see what I've found!"

The Mole hobbled up to the spot and had a good look; just peeping above the snow was a door-scraper!

The Rat set to work once more, digging down deep in the snow he discovered - a doormat!

Quick as he could Rat attacked the snow bank beside them with his stick, and Mole scraped busily away too.

After ten minutes of hard work the point of Rat's stick struck something that sounded hollow. Faster and harder they dug, until, in full view of the astonished Mole, a solid looking door appeared.

It was painted dark green. An iron bell pull hung by the side, and below it, on a small brass plate, neatly written, they could read by the aid of moonlight:

'MR. BADGER.'

The Mole fell backwards on the snow from sheer surprise and delight. "Rat!" he cried, "you're a real wonder, that's what you are!"

"Get up at once and hang on to that bell pull," ordered the Rat. "Ring as hard as you can, while I hammer."

While the Rat attacked the door with his stick, the Mole sprang up at the bell pull, clutched it and swung there, both feet off the ground, and from quite a long way off they could faintly hear a deep toned bell respond.

They waited patiently for what seemed to be a very long time, stamping in the snow to keep their feet warm. At last they heard the sound of slow shuffling footsteps approaching the door from inside.

There was the noise of a bolt shooting back and the door opened a few inches, enough to show a long snout and a pair of sleepy, blinking eyes.

"Now, who is it this time, disturbing people on such a night?" said a gruff voice.

"Oh, Badger," cried the Rat, "let us in, please. It's me, Rat, and my friend Mole, and we've lost our way in the snow."

"What, Ratty, my dear little man!" exclaimed the Badger, in quite a different voice. "Come in, both of you. You must be frozen. Well I never! Lost in the snow! And in the Wild Wood too, and at this time of night!"

The Badger, who wore a long dressing gown and slippers, had probably been on his way to bed when he heard their call.

He looked down at them kindly and patted both their heads. "This is not the sort of night for small animals to be out," he said. "Come along into the kitchen, there's a first rate fire there, and supper and everything."

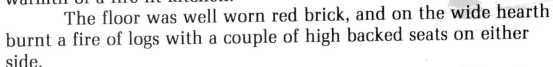

He shuffled on in front of them, carrying the light, and they followed him, nudging each other in an excited sort of way, down a long gloomy passage, until they came to several stout doors. One of which Badger flung open, and at once they found themselves in all the glow and warmth of a fire lit kitchen.

The floor was well worn red brick, and on the wide hearth burnt a fire of logs with a couple of high backed seats on either side.

In the middle of the room stood a long table with benches down each side. Rows of spotless plates winked from the shelves of the dresser, and, from the rafters overhead, hung hams, bundles of dried herbs, nets of onions and baskets of eggs.

The kindly Badger sat them down on seats to toast themselves at the fire and made them remove their wet coats and boots. Then he fetched them dressing gowns and slippers, and bathed Mole's shin with warm water.

Warm and dry at last, it seemed that the Wild Wood they had just left outside was miles and miles away.

When at last, they were thoroughly toasted, the Badger called them to the table where he had been busy laying a meal.

He sat in his armchair at the head of the table as they ate their supper. Then he listened as Ratty and Mole told of their adventures that night in the Wild Wood, and soon Mole began to feel that Badger was quite a friendly type really!

When supper was finished they chatted a while, sitting together in the firelight.

Although it was getting rather late, the Mole felt quite lively and wide awake, but the poor, tired Water Rat was worn out and kept nodding off in the Badger's warm kitchen.

"It's time we were all in bed," said Badger, getting up and fetching candlesticks. "Take your time getting up tomorrow morning - breakfast at any hour you please!"

He led the animals to a long room that seemed half bedroom and half loft. The Badger's winter stores were everywhere. They took up half the room: piles of apples, turnips, potatoes, baskets full of nuts, and jars of honey. But two little beds on the remainder of the floor looked soft and inviting, and the bed linen on them was clean and smelt of lavender. The Mole and the Water Rat shook off their clothes and tumbled in between the sheets with great joy and contentment.

When the two tired animals came down to breakfast very late next morning, they found two young hedgehogs sitting on a bench at the table, eating porridge out of wooden bowls.

"Where have you youngsters come from? Lost your way in the snow, I suppose?" the Rat asked pleasantly.

"Yes, please, sir," said the elder of the two hedgehogs respectfully. "Me and little Billy was trying to find our way to school, and Billy got frightened and cried. And at last we came and knocked on Mr. Badger's back door. For everyone knows he's such a kind hearted gentleman!"

"I understand," said Rat, cutting himself some rashers from a side of bacon, while Mole dropped some eggs into a pan. "What's the weather like outside?"

"Oh, terrible bad, sir, terrible deep the snow is!" said the hedgehog.

Suddenly the front door bell clanged loudly, and the Rat, who was very greasy with buttered toast, sent Billy, the smaller hedgehog, to see who it might be.

There was the sound of much stamping in the hall and Billy returned with the Otter, who was delighted to see Ratty and Mole safe and sound.

"Thought I'd find you here alright," said the Otter cheerfully. "Everyone on the River Bank was very worried about you both," the Otter went on. "Ratty never been home all night - nor Mole either - something dreadful must have happened, they said, and the snow had covered up all your tracks. So I came straight here to Badger's house, through the Wild Wood and the snow. My! It was fine coming through the snow, every now and then masses of snow slid off the branches, making me jump and run for cover. Snow castles and snow caverns had sprung up over night - I could have stayed and played with them for hours. Then I met a rabbit sitting on a stump. He was such a silly fellow, I had to cuff him round the ears to get any sense out of him. The rabbits in the Wild Wood knew very well that you were lost and Mole was hurt - why didn't they do something to help?"

"Weren't you at all - er - nervous?" asked the Mole remembering yesterday's terror in the Wild Wood.

"Nervous?" The Otter showed a gleaming set of strong, white teeth as he laughed. "I'd give `em nerves if any of them tried anything on with me. Here, Mole, fry me some slices of ham. I'm terribly hungry, and I've got a lot to say to Ratty, haven't seen him for ages!"

So Mole cut some slices of ham and told the hedgehogs to fry it, and returned to his own breakfast.

Badger, who had been asleep in his study, was pleased to see the Otter and invited him to lunch.

"Here, you two youngsters, be off home to your mother!" said Badger kindly to the two young hedgehogs, as he gave them sixpence each and patted their heads, and sent someone to show them the way.

All during that morning the four friends talked and talked. Then they sat down to lunch together, and afterwards they talked some more!

The Otter and the Rat settled down to talk about their beloved River Bank while Badger lit a lantern and took Mole on a tour down the dim passages of his underground home.

Now Mole was naturally an underground animal by birth, and Badger's house suited him exactly, and made him feel at home - but not the Water Rat!

When they got back to the kitchen they found him walking up and down, very restless, longing to get back to his River Bank.

So he had his overcoat on, and his pistols thrust into his belt again. "Come along, Mole," he said, as soon as he caught a sight of them. "We must get off while it's daylight. Don't want to spend another night in the Wild Wood again."

"You really needn't fret, Ratty," said the Badger. "My passages run further than you think. In fact some of them run beneath the wood, right to the very edge."

The Rat was so eager to be off, that Badger took his lantern and led the way through a maze of tunnels, until, at last, daylight began to show itself through the mouth of the passage.

Badger bade the three friends a hasty goodbye and pushed them through the opening.

They found themselves standing on the very edge of the Wild Wood. Rocks and brambles and tree-roots behind them; in front a great space of quiet fields and, far ahead, a glint of the old familiar river.

The Otter, knowing all the paths, took charge of the party, and they trailed out on a bee-line for a distant stile.

Looking back, they saw the Wild Wood, dark and menacing, behind them.

Together they turned and made for home, for firelight, and for the voice of the River that they knew and trusted, sounding cheerily outside their window.